Taneesha's
Treasures of the Heart

by
M. LaVora Perry

illustrated by
Chris R. Seaman

DORRANCE PUBLISHING CO., INC.
PITTSBURGH PENNSYLVANIA 15222

Second Printing
For information or to order additional books, please write:
Dorrance Publishing Co., Inc.
701 Smithfield Street
Pittsburgh, Pennsylvania 15222
U.S.A.
1-800-788-7654
Or visit our Web site and on-line catalog at *www.dorrancepublishing.com*

For all young people trying to keep hurtfulness out of your lives, and for Daisaku Ikeda, who taught me that I am a Buddha.

With special thanks to...
Cedric, Nia, Jarod, Jahci, Ameer, Jeff, Elder Rudolph Sr. & Mattie M. Perry, Michele Vrooman Kennett, Nancy Levin, Patricia Blochowiak, MD, & the many others who believed in this story.
-M. L. P.

Thanks to all the wonderful new friends I have made while illustrating this book: Quinn, O'nisha, Mattie, Bill, Raoul, Ruth, and Jody. Special thanks to LaVora for writing such a beautiful story—without you this wouldn't have been possible! Most of all, thanks to my parents, Mike and Rhonda, for your continued support.
-C.R.S.

Contents

Acknowledgment

The quotation from *The Writings of Nichiren Daishonin*, "Treasures of the heart are the most valuable of all," appears courtesy of the Soka Gakkai, Tokyo (copyright Soka Gakkai, 1999). The Victory Over Violence (VOV) sunflower logo and excerpts from the VOV pledge appear courtesy of Soka Gakkai International-USA (SGI-USA), Santa Monica.

A Note to Readers

There are many different religions in the world. Some people are Christian; some are Jewish, Islamic or other faiths. Some people do not practice a religion, but they hold beliefs deep in their hearts. Although people may pray in different ways, or not at all, everyone shares the great wish for peace and happiness.

Taneesha Bey-Ross is a girl whose family practices the Buddhist religion. This is her story.

The glossary at the end of the story gives the meaning and history of the Buddhist words in this book.

After school, best friends Taneesha Bey-Ross and Carli Flanagan did their fourth-grade homework.

Chapter One
Sunny Day

After school best friends Taneesha Bey-Ross and Carli Flanagan did their fourth-grade homework. They stretched, tummies down, across a snuggly purple rug. Taneesha's off-black kinky hair was braided into two neat ponytails. Freckly Carli's auburn waves fell around her face. Every now and then, she reached under the plastic and steel brace she wore on her left leg. Then she gave her knee a long scratching.

The girls were in the family library at Taneesha's cozy, old-fashioned house in East Cleveland, Ohio. Every so often, through the entryway, Taneesha glimpsed shimmering sunrays dancing on the polished cherry wood of the Bey-Ross's altar. The altar was in the living room, which was next to the library.

Taneesha's father was named Miles and her mother was Alima. Each morning and evening they sit before the altar to recite parts of the Lotus Sutra scripture. Along with their recitation, they chant the words, Nam-myoho-renge-kyo. As Nichiren Buddhists, chanting is how they pray.

In time Taneesha heard keys jingling in the kitchen door. She knew they were Daddy's because it was Tuesday. On Tuesdays he always arrived home from his office about fifteen minutes after she got in from school. Daddy has his own financial advisement firm. As a financial advisor, he explains ways that people can use their money wisely. Taneesha ran to greet him at the door.

"Hey Daddy, how was work?" Taneesha asked, hugging Daddy around the middle. The wavy naps of his shiny ebony hair looked freshly cut to Taneesha. She felt the itchy bristles of his mustache as he leaned over to hug her back warmly.

"Great, sweetie," Daddy smiled. "Ready for some hot chocolate and a snack before I get started on dinner?"

"Yes please," answered Taneesha. "Carli's probably gonna want some too."

Daddy acted surprised, asking "Oh? Little Miss Flanagan's here?" Taneesha knew he was only kidding around, because she and Carli almost always studied together. "Hi, Carli!" he called from the hallway. "Come on in the kitchen for some hot chocolate, dear!"

Soon, Taneesha, Carli, and Daddy sat at the kitchen table. They sipped from warm mugs, munched from a popcorn bowl, and chomped carrots and celery sticks dipped in peanut butter.

Between mouthfuls, Daddy said, "You girls are like paper and ink, you're so close. Try to stay that way, you hear? Good friends are hard to come by. They're a real treasure of the heart. You know, in one of his letters Nichiren wrote, 'Treasures of the heart are the most valuable of all.'"

"Yeah, yeah, yeah, you've said that before, Daddy," Taneesha sighed in a sassy tone. "But I don't even know what a treasure of the heart is."

"Well first, Miz Ten-years-old-going-on-twenty-five, you two tell me this: What's a treasure?" Daddy replied, grabbing a handful of popcorn.

Taneesha thought for a moment.

Meanwhile, Carli suggested, "Well...a treasure's something that's very special and beautiful...like diamonds and gold."

"And..." Taneesha added, "...it's something you have to look for. You know, like spies do."

Daddy scooped up more fluffy kernels. "Now, considering what you both just said, what do you think a treasure of the heart is?" he quizzed.

Slowly, Carli began, "I guess...you can't really touch it...because it's inside. It's in your heart."

Taneesha joined in, "Yeah, but even though you can't touch it, it's still awesome."

"And," Carli went on, "you have to look for it, because it's not real easy to find...it's uncommon."

Daddy made a clapping sound as he brushed oily salt from his hands. He said, "Well young ladies, seems to me you've just answered your own question. A treasure of the heart is something you can't touch, that's beautiful, special, and hard to find. *Rare*," Daddy said, pointing his finger sweepingly from Carli to Taneesha, "*that's* what your friendship is," he announced with a jab in the air. "Please always remember what a wonderful thing you have. Stand by each other on the cloudy days, not just the sunny ones, okay?"

"Okie dokey, Daddy," Taneesha said in her goofiest voice, thinking, *Oh boy, Daddy's so dramatic sometimes.*

"We'll stick together, Mr. Bey-Ross," Carli chimed in, giggling at Taneesha's clowning.

Just then, a gust of chilly wind blew through the kitchen as Taneesha's mother opened the door. Taneesha knew Mama was returning from Huron Hospital where she works as a nurse.

"Hey, Mama," Taneesha smiled, admiring how melting snowflakes sparkled in her mother's natural hairstyle and on her velvety-brown skin.

A gust of chilly wind blew through the kitchen as Taneesha's mother opened the door.

Mama put her coat and purse away and washed her hands in the downstairs restroom. Then she came back into the kitchen. Almost as if singing, she said, "Taneesha, I've got news for you. Remember when you came to the hospital with me for Take Your Child to Work Day?"

"Yeah. I had a good time." She wondered what Mama's news could be.

"Well," Mama continued, "I was thinking about how much you really liked meeting the children with diabetes. And how much they liked you too. So...I asked my department's director if you could come by the hospital after school sometimes to read with them. And she said okay. Do you wanna do it?"

"Sure! That sounds fun!" Taneesha exclaimed. She recalled meeting lots of nice people at Mama's job. She learned new things about the disease called diabetes. Her visit to the hospital helped her understand why some people with diabetes need shots to stay healthy.

♥

Later, after the girls finished their homework, Taneesha heard the honk of Mr. Flanagan's car horn. She knew he had come to take Carli home.

"Well, that's Papa," Carli said, gathering her books while

Taneesha looked on. "Gotta go now."

Soon Carli was out the door. Taneesha and Daddy stood waving at the living room window as Mr. Flanagan backed his car out of the driveway.

Then Daddy turned to Taneesha and smiled. "Ready to do our evening prayer?" he asked. "By the time we're through, dinner should be ready."

"Naw, I'll pass, Daddy," Taneesha yawned. "I just want to take a little nap. It's been a long day."

Chapter Two
Cloudy Day

The following morning the sky was overcast, and Taneesha overslept. She arrived late to Chambers Elementary School. In her classroom, she scurried to put her outerwear away and get to her desk, which was next to Carli's.

Carli grinned, whispering, "Hey, girl!" as Taneesha sat down.

Winded from rushing all the way to school, Taneesha smiled at Carli. She swallowed the last bit of bagel that she had gobbled along the way. Then she responded breathlessly, "Hey…girl."

"Good to see you this morning, Ms. Bey-Ross," said Taneesha's teacher, Mr. Ying, from his desk. Peering at her over the top of his rectangular gold-rimmed glasses, he asked, "Did you sign in at the office?"

"Yes, Mr. Ying."

Ronnie, who sat in front of Taneesha, turned slightly toward her, smirking. He whispered, "Why you late, Taneesha? Stayed home chantin' to pass today's social studies test?"

Rolling her eyes, Taneesha said, "No, I'm just late, that's all."

"Well, throw some nam-yo-yo's my way, okay?" Ronnie joked. "I need all the luck I can get!"

"Boy, you are *so* silly," Taneesha giggled under her breath.

Mr. Ying loudly cleared his throat. "Taneesha, you're already tardy," he warned. "You'd do well to stop talking and start your class work."

"Yes, Mr. Ying," Taneesha sheepishly replied.

"Boy, you are so *silly," Taneesha giggled under her breath.*

She slinked down into her seat, wishing she could disappear. She raised her desktop and ducked her head inside to hide. She didn't dare look at anyone, not even Carli. She removed her notebook and pencil. She closed her desk, read the lesson off the chalkboard, and began writing.

♥

At the end of the school day, Taneesha and Carli laughed, slowly making their way to Taneesha's house. In fun, they tossed snowballs at each other. Suddenly, someone snickered, "Hey you! What's up with your leg? Is it broke?"

Taneesha turned around to find a bigger, older girl standing over Carli. Taneesha saw that Carli must have just slipped onto the sidewalk. She helped her to her feet. The two friends stood side by side as Carli brushed snow from her coat.

Carli answered the older girl, "No, my leg's not broken. It got messed up a little when I was a baby, but I'm okay now. I just have to wear a brace to help me walk."

Taneesha knew all about what happened to Carli. Mr. Flanagan had told her one day when the girls were still in kindergarten. He said Carli and her mother were in a bad car crash. That's when Carli's mother died. Now Taneesha remembered the tears in Mr. Flanagan's eyes when he spoke about the accident.

"What do you mean you gotta wear a brace to help you walk?" the older girl asked. "You mean you a cripple, right?" She broke into laughter. She pointed to Carli's leg, shouting, "Hey, you ain't nothin' but a little cripple, girl!"

"I am *not* a cripple!" Carli yelled back. "I just wear a brace, that's all!"

Taneesha fumed as Carli's words drowned in the older girl's loud laughter. She demanded, "You leave her alone!" Her chest echoed the pounding beat of her heart. "She hasn't done anything to you! You're being mean and stupid!"

Taneesha and the older girl glared at each other, standing

Taneesha stumbled backwards, falling down, almost into the street.

frozen in place.

Carli gently took Taneesha's hand, saying, "Let's just go home, Taneesha. It's okay. I'm all right."

"Oh yeah?" snarled the older girl, "Well, I don't like the way your friend here just spoke to me, little cripple girl."

"She's *not* a cripple," insisted Taneesha. "She has a name. You shouldn't call people ugly names. You wouldn't like it if somebody called *you* one."

"Is that right? Well, what you gonna do about it?" said the older girl, pushing Taneesha's shoulder.

Taneesha stumbled backwards, falling down, almost into the street. Carli gasped. She helped Taneesha to her feet. The older girl reached to shove Taneesha again, when...

"Surprise! Hey, hop in girls!" Taneesha was so glad to see that Mama had pulled up along the curb in her minivan. "I got off work a little early today, so I came by to pick you two up," said Mama brightly.

"Don't think it's *over*! I'll be back for *you*," spat the older girl through clenched teeth. Taneesha and Carli quickly walked by her. The older girl whispered angrily to Taneesha, "No little kid's gonna talk to *me* like that!"

Chapter Three
Turning Things Around

Taneesha and Carli leaped into the middle-row seats of the minivan.

"Mama, she was pushing me!" Taneesha panted.

"She called me a 'cripple'!" added Carli.

"She's gonna *get* me, Mama!"

"We didn't do anything to her!" explained Carli.

"Wait, wait! I can't understand a word you're saying," replied Mama as she eased the minivan into the driving lane. "Slow down, and tell me one at a time, okay?"

Taneesha blurted out breathlessly, "Mama, that big old girl started picking on Carli. And when I told her to stop, she got all mad at me, and now she says she's gonna *get* me. She called Carli a 'cripple,' Mama. She shouldn't've done that, right? Daddy told me to stick by my friend. Well, I did; now I'm gonna get *beat up*!"

"I'm sorry, Taneesha," apologized Carli. "I'm sorry I've gotten you into trouble."

Taneesha gave Carli's shoulder a gentle squeeze. "It's not your fault, Carli," she said. "That girl was wrong. I just don't know what I'm gonna do, that's all. Mama, what am I gonna *do*?"

"First of all," Mama answered, "calm down and take a good, deep breath."

"Hhhuuuuuuhhh...whhhooooooohhh," blew voicelessly from everyone's lips.

"Second of all," continued Mama, "you know what *I* think you should do, don't you?"

"Pray?" Taneesha asked, knowing Mama had the same answer for everything.

"You got it," Mama answered.

Still upset, Taneesha asked, "But, Mama, this is *reality*. What if I get *beat up*?!"

"Hey, that's not going to happen," promised Mama. "Tomorrow I'll come by again to pick you both up after school. If the girl's around, I'll have a talk with her."

Taneesha was frightened. She caught Mama's eye in the rearview mirror.

"Now don't you worry," assured Mama. "I'll make sure that girl leaves you alone. If I've got to talk to the principal, her parents, or whatever, I'll do it. But you should still pray, sweetheart. Then you'll start feeling like a **fearless lion queen**." Mama said 'fearless lion queen' in a fake super-hero voice, making Taneesha and Carli laugh in spite of themselves.

Still chuckling a little, Carli asked, "Prayer can do all that?"

"Sure can, Carli," Mama replied.

Taneesha saw Mama's smile through the rearview mirror.

"Can I try it too?" asked Carli.

Taneesha shot a surprised look at Carli, wondering, *Did I hear right? Since when is Carli so interested in praying?*

"Tell you what, Carli," Mama answered, "when we get to the house, why don't you call your father and ask him? Let him know what happened today. If he says it's all right for you to chant with us this afternoon, you're more than welcome."

For the rest of the ride home Taneesha never parted her lips. She was too busy thinking about how Mama and Daddy kept praying even when the worst happened. She thought about how they always managed to turn things around.

"Come on, Taneesha." Taneesha looked up to find Mama standing at the open minivan door. "Get on out, honey."

Taneesha hadn't noticed Mama turning into her family's driveway. Startled, she jumped out of the minivan and darted into the house. She scuttled to hang up her hat and coat. Then she opened the large oval cabinet that rested atop the altar table. She sat down in the chair in front of the altar.

She pulled open the slender altar table drawer and took out her plastic lavender prayer beads. From off the table, she picked up the slickly lacquered, black-handled wooden mallet. The

Taneesha thought about the way Mama and Daddy always managed to turn things around.

mallet's top was covered with soft, white leather. On the floor next to her chair sat a wooden pedestal topped with a purple pillow. A potbelly black metal bell sat on the pillow. Using a steady swing, Taneesha struck the shiny bell with the mallet. Bong! Bong! Bonnnnnnnnnnnnng! echoed through the house.

As the sound of the bell drifted away, Taneesha sensed Mama standing quietly next to her. Mama lit the candle on the altar, smiled lovingly at Taneesha, then turned and walked out of the room.

Taneesha placed the prayer beads over her fingers. The fuzzy white cloth balls on their ends dangled from the back of her hands. She sat straight and tall. She gazed slightly upward at the words written on the scroll that hung from a brass hook inside the altar cabinet. The creamy-white paper scroll, framed by a golden green cloth, was her family's Gohonzon. In bold black-ink brushstrokes of Chinese letters, the words Nam-myoho-renge-kyo flowed down the center of the Gohonzon.

Taneesha pressed her palms together and held them in front of her chest. She chanted "Nam-myoho-renge-kyo" three times very slowly. Then she quickened her pace to a galloping "Nam-myoho-renge-kyo…Nam-myoho-renge-kyo…Nam-myoho-renge-kyo…." She felt calm warmth start to glow from within. The warmth soon spread all over her. Her body and mind joined the rhythm of her voice. She relaxed, feeling strong and powerful.

Meanwhile, Carli called Mr. Flanagan on the telephone.

Soon Taneesha heard Carli sob, "I feel so *awful*, Papa. Taneesha's my best friend, and now she's in big trouble, all

Taneesha chanted Nam-myoho-renge-kyo three times very slowly.

because of *me*!"

Taneesha prayed harder.

Carli sniffled, "Okay Papa, I won't be so tough on myself. I'm glad you're gonna be there tomorrow. Ms. Bey-Ross is coming too.

"Oh, Papa," continued Carli, "there's something I wanted to ask you. Taneesha's chanting right now. Can I do it too?" After a few moments, Taneesha heard Carli squeal, "I *can*?! Thanks, Papa! Bye!"

Carli hung up the telephone and hurriedly sat down next to Taneesha. She told her excitedly, "My father says he really respects your family a lot. He says he doesn't think your mother would ask me to do anything wrong. So he says if I really want to try it out, *I can!*"

"Great!" exclaimed Taneesha. She showed Carli how to chant.

At first, as she chanted, all Taneesha imagined was not getting beat up. But after a while, she remembered something.

"You know what, Carli? We oughtta chant for that girl to be happy."

"What? *Why?*" puzzled Carli. "She was so mean to us."

"I know," Taneesha agreed, "but maybe she wouldn't be mean if she was happy. Anyway, my parents always say it's good to pray for people's happiness."

"Oh all right," Carli halfheartedly shrugged.

As they continued to chant, Taneesha was so focused that she didn't even notice when Daddy returned home from work.

In time, the girls recited the Lotus Sutra with Mama and Daddy. Taneesha pointed out the scripture's words in her sutra book for Carli.

Afterwards, Taneesha and Carli started their homework. When they finished, Carli stayed for dinner. Then the time came for Daddy and Taneesha to take Carli home.

♥

When they arrived at Carli's house, Daddy knocked on the door. Opening the door with a concerned look on his face, Mr. Flanagan said, "Good evening everybody."

"Good evening, Liam," Daddy replied.

"Good evening, Mr. Flanagan."

"Hi, Papa."

"I guess our young ladies have themselves a problem, huh?" Mr. Flanagan continued. Taneesha watched him tenderly pat Carli's head. She waved goodbye while Carli walked inside. She looked up as Mr. Flanagan addressed Daddy saying, "I'll be meeting them after school tomorrow. Is Alima still doing the same?"

Daddy answered, "Yes she is."

"Good, good," said Mr. Flanagan. "We gotta keep this thing from getting out of hand. We can't have some big kid bullying our girls....By the way," he went on, "Carli asked me if she could do that chanting you all do. How'd that go?"

"Great!" chirped Taneesha. "We chanted *a lot*!"

Opening the door with a concerned look on his face, Mr. Flanagan said, "Good evening, everybody."

Taneesha noticed Mr. Flanagan smiling a little when he said, "You know, my late wife, Pearl, used to do some meditating herself. Is that what you do?"

"Well," Daddy said, "somewhat maybe, but it's different, too.... It's the kind of thing you gotta try out for yourself to really understand. But listen, when we've got a little more time, we can talk about it."

To Taneesha, Mr. Flanagan seemed lost in thought. "Yeah," he began, "Pearl was always trying to get me into that meditation stuff...but I was never real big on that kind of thing.... I guess I've been sorta missing all that..."

Taneesha tried hard to hear him, but Mr. Flanagan's words trailed off.

Chapter Four
Bullies Have Feelings

The next day at lunch, Taneesha and Carli sat together in the school cafeteria. From her seat, Taneesha looked out the window at the cloudy gray day.

Carli asked, "What if our parents don't make it in time? What if that girl beats you up and me too?"

"Well, I got up early today to do my morning prayer with my parents," Taneesha responded. She

"Well, I got up early today..." Taneesha responded. She tried to keep a brave smile on her face.

tried to keep a brave smile on her face. "And my mother says she's coming." Carli's questions were making Taneesha imagine Mama and Mr. Flanagan being late. She felt her stomach churn and she winced, picturing the older girl punching her in the face. Then she blinked hard, snapping back to the present. She sat up straight in her seat and said, "Anyway, I'm trying to think positive."

"Yeah?" Carli asked. "Well, I chanted with my father too. Before school he wanted me to show him how."

"Good." Taneesha saw the troubled look on Carli's face. "We'll be all right, okay?" she assured, warmly patting Carli's hand.

"Okay. If you say so," replied Carli.

♥

Before long, school was over. Taneesha and Carli stood outside the building shivering in the winter cold, waiting for their parents.

"Uh, oh," said Carli nervously, "Guess who's coming across the street?"

Taneesha turned toward the direction in which Carli was looking. She saw the older girl approaching from the crosswalk near where she and Carli waited. As the older girl walked closer, she didn't take her angry stare off Taneesha for a second.

Time stopped for Taneesha. She understood what was happening, but she was surprised to realize that she wasn't at all afraid. She stood still and ready to grab Carli's hand and take off down the street if she needed to. She watched the older girl come nearer.

With her eyes glued to Taneesha, the older girl stepped over the curb. Then, unexpectedly, she tripped over a clump of snow. Losing her balance, she fell forward onto the shoveled sidewalk. In an instant, Taneesha and Carli bent down to help her up.

"Get away from me!" the older girl barked. "I don't need y'all's help!" Struggling, she made it to her feet and began brushing dirt and snow off her coat. After straightening out her backpack book bag, she looked toward the ground. As if noticing something there, she quickly stooped down. She picked up a small blue pouch from the sidewalk. Taneesha saw that two little medical needles and a blood sugar meter had fallen from the drawstring opening of the pouch. She recognized these items from her visit to Huron Hospital for Take Your Child to Work Day.

Glancing sideways at Taneesha, the older girl snatched up the needles and blood sugar meter. She then swiftly shook them down into the pouch and drew the pouch closed. She pulled her backpack frontward along her side. She tucked the pouch into a side backpack pocket. She zippered the pocket, pushed her backpack into place behind her, and then glowered at Taneesha and Carli. She asked sharply, "What y'all looking at?"

In her mind, Taneesha pictured Mama at work helping patients give themselves shots. They used the same kind of needles the older girl had. She faced the older girl and asked

Losing her balance, the older girl fell forward onto the shoveled sidewalk.

with concern, "Do you have diabetes?"

"Taneesha, let's just walk away," Carli urged. "Don't ask her any funny questions."

The older girl snarled, "None of your business what I got." Then, with her scowl softening a bit, she asked, "And anyway, what do you know about diabetes?"

"My mother's a nurse," Taneesha answered. "I've seen people with diabetes at her hospital. I even met a doctor who has it. I know sometimes people with diabetes have to get shots so they won't get sick. Is that why you have needles?"

"You seen a doctor with diabetes?" the older girl questioned doubtfully.

"Yup. Dr. Inez Ortega," Taneesha replied. "She's real nice, too. My mother says people with diabetes have to take their medicine when they're supposed to, eat right, and exercise. Then they can do the same things as everybody else."

"What's it like having diabetes?" Carli asked.

"I'm just finding out myself," confessed the older girl. "I got it all of a sudden. The doctor says my body don't use sugar like it's supposed to. All I know is I can't eat like normal people." She looked downward, then quietly said, "Y'all probably wanna laugh at me, right?"

Taneesha and Carli slowly shook their heads no.

The older girl seemed relieved. She said, "I don't know about those people at your mother's job. But *I sure* hate having to take a buncha stupid shots all the time. I was scared if anybody found out I'm sick they'd think I'm weird. So I ain't told none of my friends."

Carli told her, "Well, if they're really your friends, they won't mind if you're different. Real friends stick by each other, no matter what."

Taneesha agreed. "Yeah, that's 'cause a real friend's a treasure..." gently patting her own chest with a fuzzy-mittened hand, she said, "...*right here*, inside your heart."

"Sometimes," the older girl nearly whispered, "I even get scared I'm gonna die 'cause I got a dumb disease."

The three of them stood silently as a light snow began to fall. Snowflakes gently melted on their cheeks.

"But *you* know a doctor with diabetes," the older girl said to Taneesha. "So I could live a long time with it too—just like her." The older girl looked downward. She seemed to Taneesha to be thinking hard. Then she raised her eyes until they met Taneesha's eyes and Carli's. She said, "Sorry I was so mean to y'all yesterday. I guess I was in kind of a bad mood."

"That's okay. I get in bad moods too, sometimes," comforted Taneesha.

"Yeah, me too," Carli added.

"Um...my name's...my name's Jewel," said the older girl.

Taneesha and Carli beamed, "I'm Taneesha," and "I'm Carli."

Just then, Taneesha saw Mr. Flanagan's car, followed by Mama's minivan, pull up speedily along the curb. Their windows slid down.

"Taneesha, you all right?" Mama called anxiously.

"Is everything okay, Carli?" hollered Mr. Flanagan.

"We're fine!" Taneesha and Carli both answered, grinning broadly.

All at once, the sun sailed from behind a cloud and scattered shimmering beads of light on the falling snowflakes. Taneesha felt warm from the inside out. The whole world seemed to shine especially for her.

She looked at Carli. The two friends smiled joyfully at each other, and then they smiled at Jewel too. Together Taneesha and Carli turned and waved to their parents saying, "See you at home!"

Together, Taneesha and Carli turned and waved to their parents saying, "See you at home!"

Glossary

Altar (ALL-ter): A piece of furniture, such as a table, that a person sits or kneels in front of to pray.

Buddha (BOO-duh): Buddha is a word from an ancient Indian language called Sanskrit. It means someone who sees the limitless greatness of the universe within all life and things.

Buddhist (BOO-dist): Someone who follows the teachings of a religion called Buddhism (BOO-diz-um). Buddhism was started by a man named Siddhartha Gautama (Sid-AR-tah GOT-uh-muh). He was also called Shakyamuni (SHOCK-yah-moo-nee), or simply the Buddha. The Buddha lived in India about 3,000 years ago. He preached a lot of different teachings to help people become happy. All of the Buddha's teachings, along with those of many of his followers, are known as Buddhism.

Chant (Chant): To rhythmically say a word, phrase, or sentence over and over.

Gohonzon (GO-hone-zone): A paper scroll with a white background that has Nam-myoho-renge-kyo written down the center in bold black-ink Chinese letters. Nichiren created the first Gohonzon. Nichiren Buddhists focus on the words on the Gohonzon when they chant Nam-myoho-renge-kyo. They keep Gohonzon that look like the original one Nichiren created in their altars at home.

In Japanese, Gohonzon means "Object of Fundamental Respect and Devotion." Nichiren taught that the Gohonzon is a type of mirror. He said that chanting before it helps anyone see that his or her life is always respect worthy and great.

Lotus Sutra (LO-tus SOO-tra): Lotuses are lovely flowers that grow and bloom in muddy water. They are also called water lillies. Sutra is a word from the ancient Indian language called Sanskrit. It means a teaching of the Buddha.

In the Lotus Sutra the Buddha taught that people are like lotus flowers. He said that people's problems and worries are like muddy swamps where lotus flowers grow. By this he meant that all people are originally beautiful Buddhas who can turn any problems into wonderful benefits. He said each person has unlimited power inside to make her or his every dream come true.

The Buddha called the Lotus Sutra his greatest teaching. Myoho-renge-kyo is a Japanese way to say Lotus Sutra. Each morning and evening, Nichiren Buddhists recite part of the Lotus Sutra and chant the words Nam-myoho-renge-kyo.

Nam-myoho-renge-kyo (N'ah'm-m'yo-ho-ren-geh-k'yo):
Nam is a word from the ancient Indian language called
Sanskrit. It means, "I devote my life to." Nam-myoho-renge-
kyo means, "I devote my life to the Mystic Law of the Lotus
Flower teaching of the Buddha."

Nichiren Buddhists believe that Nam-myoho-renge-kyo
also has a deeper meaning than words can explain. They call
it the Mystic Law of Life, and they pray by chanting Nam-
myoho-renge-kyo. They believe Nam-myoho-renge-kyo is
the great happiness that is within and connects all people,
animals, and things. Everyday they chant to bring this
happiness out of their lives.

This happiness is also called Enlightenment (In-LIGHT-
en-ment) or Buddhaood (BOO-duh-hood). This happiness is
said to light up people's lives so they see the Buddha within
themselves and within all others.

Nichiren Buddhism (NEE-chee-ren): The Buddhism
founded by Nichiren. Nichiren was a thirteenth century
Japanese Buddhist teacher. He taught many people to chant
Nam-myoho-renge-kyo—this started a new kind of
Buddhism. Nichiren also created the original Gohonzon.

Recite (ri-SITE): To rhythmically read or say words by
memory out loud.

Scripture (SKRIP-chur): The written teachings of a
religion.

Soka Gakkai International (SO-kah GAH-kye): Also called the SGI, and in the United States of America, the SGI-USA. Soka Gakkai is Japanese for "The Society for Creating Value." The SGI is a lay organization of Nichiren Buddhists with members in about 200 countries. The SGI is a non-governmental member of the United Nations. SGI members work for peace, culture, and education. They join people of many different beliefs to create a better world.

No More Hurtfulness "VICTORY OVER VIOLENCE"

Victory means winning. Violence means hurting. The bullying that takes place in *Taneesha's Treasures of the Heart* is a type of violence. In 1999, young people in the Soka Gakkai International-USA (SGI-USA) started "Victory Over Violence" (VOV). They wanted to help other youths be winners who stop hurtful unkindness in their lives and communities.

VOV is for people of all beliefs. There have been many VOV programs and activities at schools and in neighborhoods all around the United States.

If you would like to have VOV at your school or in your community, call the SGI-USA at (310) 260-8900. You will find out how to get in touch with someone who knows about VOV in your hometown. You can also learn more about VOV and print out directions for activities from the Web at www.vov.com.

from the VOV Pledge

I will value my own life.

I will never give up on my dreams, even if they seem impossible.

I will respect all life.

I will inspire hope in others.

Healthy Habits

Taneesha learned about diabetes in the hospital where her mother works as a nurse. She probably learned that your body makes something called insulin. Insulin helps turn sugar and other foods into energy. When you have the disease called diabetes, your body does not make or use insulin correctly.

If diabetes runs in your family, you might be more likely to get it. However, doctors say there are two big reasons why more and more children and adults are getting diabetes today: Too many people are overweight and do not exercise enough.

To keep your body, mind, and spirit in good shape, some health professionals (like doctors and nurses) suggest these habits:

- Ask health professionals questions about your health.
- Read books about good health habits.
- Pray or meditate and/or think positive thoughts about yourself and others.
- Treat yourself, all people, animals, and the earth with kindness and respect.

- Follow health and safety rules. For example, wash your hands before eating and wear seatbelts in cars.
- Help others.
- Set goals for what you want to do in your life, and work to meet your goals.
- Try to improve yourself everyday, even if just a little.
- Limit soft drinks and fruit juices—your body does not need the extra sugar.
- Drink plenty of water all day long.
- Limit starchy foods (like potatoes, white bread, and white rice). Your body quickly turns them into sugar.
- Eat whole grains (like oatmeal, whole grain bread, and brown rice).
- Limit junk, fast, fatty, sugary, and salty foods (like sweets, chips, burgers, and fried foods).
- Say yes to lots of fresh plant foods (like vegetables, beans, nuts, seeds, and fruits).
- Notice how much food you are eating; only eat when you are hungry.
- Limit milk and milk products (like cheese, ice cream, and milkshakes). They might upset your stomach.
- Try soymilk, soy, and rice cheeses and other substitutes for milk and meat (like tofu).
- Eating turkey, chicken, and fish is okay.
- Eating lots of red meat (like beef and pork) is not okay.
- Exercise your body everyday—walk, run, jump, dance, and play games that use a lot of energy. Stretch your body before and after you exercise.
- Go outside to enjoy nature often.
- Be creative—for example, read, write, draw, dance, sing, enjoy lots of different types of music.
- Take a children's multivitamin every day.

- ◆ Get enough sleep—not too much or too little.
- ◆ Do not smoke, do drugs, or drink alcohol.

For more information about diabetes call the American Diabetes Association at 1-800-DIABETES (1-800-342-2383), look on the Web at www.diabetes.org, or write to the American Diabetes Association, ATTN: Customer Service, 1701 North Beauregard Street, Alexandria, VA 22311.

Books for Children, Teens, Parents, Teachers, and Others

Middleway Press books are available from local and online bookstores and on the Web at www.middlewaypress.org. All other books below can be ordered from the Soka Gakkai International–USA: www.sgi-usa.org. Tel: (310) 260-8900

For Toddlers and Preschoolers
I Like to Chant. Santa Monica: Treasure Tower Books, 2000.

For School-Aged Children
Iwamoto, Linda Jackson. *Cody Chants*. Santa Monica: Treasure Tower Books, 2000.

For Teens
Ikeda, Daisaku. *The Way of Youth: Buddhist Common Sense for Handling Life's Questions*. Santa Monica: Middleway Press, 2000.

For Parents, Teachers & Others
The Gosho Translation Committee, Editor and Translator. *The Writings of Nichiren Daishonin*. Tokyo: Soka Gakkai, 1999.

Hochswender, Woody, Martin, Greg, & Morino, Ted. *The Buddha in Your Mirror: Practical Buddhism and the Search for Self*. Santa Monica: Middleway Press, 2001.

Ikeda, Daisaku, Krieger, David & Gage, Richard L. (Translator): *Choose Hope: Your Role in Waging Peace in the Nuclear Age*. Santa Monica: Middleway Press, 2002.

Ikeda, Daisaku. *For the Sake of Peace: Seven Paths to Global Harmony—A Buddhist Perspective*. Santa Monica: Middleway Press, 2001.

Ikeda, Daisaku. *Soka Education: A Buddhist Vision for Teachers, Students and Parents*. Santa Monica: Middleway Press, 2001.

The Winning Life: An Introduction to Buddhist Practice. Santa Monica: World Tribune Press, 2000.

To learn more about Nichiren Buddhism in the United States of America contact the Soka Gakkai International-USA (SGI-USA). Soka Gakkai means "The Society for Creating Value." You can telephone the SGI-USA at (310) 260-8900; look on the Web at www.sgi-usa.org; or write: SGI-USA, 606 Wilshire Blvd, Santa Monica, CA 90406.

The SGI is a lay organization of Nichiren Buddhists with members in about 200 countries. Visit the Web site www.sgi.org for more information.

Meet The Author

© T. Darryl Polk

Author M. LaVora Perry grew up in Cleveland, Ohio and graduated from Cleveland State University's College of Education. From 1995-2002 she wrote and edited cards and calendars for American Greetings®. Her writing has appeared on gift items in the United States, Canada, the United Kingdom Australia, New Zealand and in Spanish translation in Mexico.

LaVora writes columns for "Friends for Peace"—the children's section of the *World Tribune* Buddhist newspaper. She wrote *Taneesha's Treasures of the Heart* while remembering the time she and her classmate were bullied in elementary school. Today she tries to be courageous and caring like Taneesha.

Visit LaVora's Web site at www.mlavoraperry.com or www.fortunechildbooks.com.

Meet The Illustrator

Artist Chris R. Seaman is from Canton, Ohio. In fifth grade he once had a detention for drawing pictures instead of doing class work. However, he grew up to graduate at the top of his class at the Columbus College of Art and Design.

Chris illustrated the Harry Potter® collectable card game for Wizards of the Coast® in association with Warner Brothers Studios®. He is currently illustrating new books.

© Daniel Seaman